This Orchard book

belongs to

....

TEN LITTLE UNICORNS

MIKE BROWNLOW   SIMON RICKERTY

ORCHARD

Ten little unicorns are summoned by the queen.

"The Royal Chef has disappeared. He's nowhere to be seen!

We need his birthday cake for Princess Petal's special day.

Can you help me, Unicorns?" They all say,

"NEIGH!"

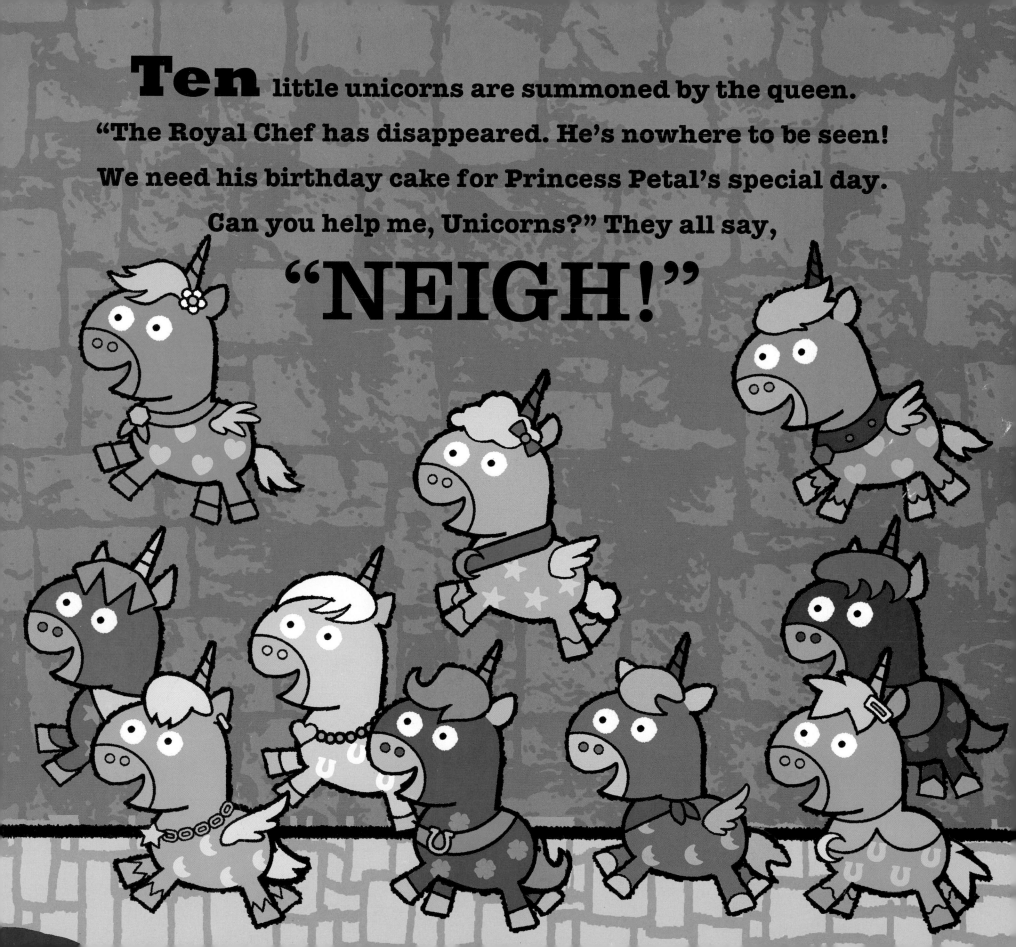

Ten little unicorns
go hunting for a sign.

10

. . . nine.

Nine little unicorns
start to levitate.

9

. . .eight.

8

Eight little unicorns – "This cottage tastes like heaven."

ZAP!

They've made the witch quite cross!

Now there are . . .

. . . **seven.**

Seven little unicorns aren't
fooled by Wolfie's tricks.

7

. . . **six.**

Six little unicorns –
the forest's come alive!

6

With lots of ghouls and ghosties!

. . . **five.**

Five little unicorns,
saved by Merlin's door.

5

SPLODGE!

Mind the pudding bowls!

Now there are . . .

... four.
Four little unicorns
search the Golden Tree.

SHUUS

4

SHHH...

Don't wake the dragon up!

Now there are . . .

...three.

Three little unicorns – that looks fun!

WOO-HOO!

3

Sliding down the rainbow –

WHEEEE!

Now there are . . .

. . . two.

**Two little unicorns ask,
"Where's the Royal Chef gone?"**

2

SPLOSH! The Frog Prince doesn't know. Now there's only . . .

. . . one.

One little unicorn, sad and in despair.
The Royal Chef's still missing and
they've hunted everywhere.

1

But then the little unicorn
makes out a tiny sound.

A voice is shouting, "LET ME OUT!"
from somewhere underground . . .

She opens up a hidden
door and there he is – hooray!
"Thank you!" says the chef, "Cos
I've been trapped down here ALL DAY!

I thought I'd hide the cake so it
would be a big surprise."

"But then the door blew shut and no one seemed to hear my cries.

The guests will all be waiting, but the cake is quite a weight.

Can you help me unicorn? I hope we're not too late!"

Princess Petal has arrived,

and all her guests as well.

Here's the cake! WOW! What a sight!

And what a tale to tell!

"Thank you," says the queen,

"for you have really saved the day!"

Ten little unicorns all say,

"NEIGH!"

For Emily and Toby, with thanks for all their unicorn advice.
And for Rex, Polly and Rowan too! – M.B.

For Cassandra – my magical Unicorn – love you X – S.R.

ORCHARD BOOKS

First published in Great Britain in 2021 by The Watts Publishing Group

1 3 5 7 9 10 8 6 4 2

Text © Mike Brownlow, 2021
Illustrations © Simon Rickerty, 2021

A CIP catalogue record for this book is available from the British Library.

ISBN 978 1 40835 591 6

Printed and bound in China

Orchard Books
An imprint of Hachette Children's Group
Part of The Watts Publishing Group Limited
Carmelite House
50 Victoria Embankment
London EC4Y 0DZ

An Hachette UK Company
www.hachette.co.uk

www.hachettechildrens.co.uk